WHO'S THE MASTER

ERIC REESE

ISBN: 978-1-925988-29-1

*For my family unknown taken from a land
known to a place unknown!*

CONTENTS

The chains were so tight that it felt as if it would rip Miro's wrists apart while the heat burned her cheeks, making her head feel heavy. She was scared as she maintained marching in a straight line, without a clue where she was headed. It was exceptionally warm that day with no signs of clouds. It was something, she dearly missed but not as much as her freedom. *Will the young woman ever experience such again in her country of Senegal?* Curious, she peeped to her right, only to discover a line was so long she could barely see its end. The men and women were shackled together. Every time she turned, a man on a horse would threaten her with a foreign object; a long cord fastened to a handle. By his garments, the man was an outsider with a smelly scent.

Loud cries were heard afar making Miro eager to turn around again. This time she was caught and got struck on the back by that man with the foreign object. Yelping in horror, the pain was too much to bear. Miro had never experienced such agony. Her back burned but not everyone around her seemed to be fazed, as they were too scared to lift their heads. She was scared and kept on walking as commanded knowing wherever she was heading, it wouldn't be a pleasant place. They approached the end of a hill and her legs were giving up on her slowly. Hours of walking in the sun made her skin toughen.

From a distance, Miro spotted a large vessel with three squared masts and a full bowsprit. As the group got closer, they were forced to move faster.

One by one they were pushed inside to the lowest part. There wasn't enough space for so many of her people. Endless cries echoed through the wooden partitions; a terror of uncertainty and desperation. In front of Miro, there was an old woman being whipped many times. Her head fell to the floor and she put her arms around it to protect herself. "What was the use?" thought Miro. The hopes of escaping were little to none.

More were pushed in, leaving little room and it appeared they were the last. Miro remained calm despite the madness happening. Her mind traveled back to her family. The looks on their faces when many of her relatives were being dragged away. Her father was executed because he rebelled. Now, there's a possibility they would never see each other again. Miro got away by the help of her mother, but was quickly captured. Her mother's whereabouts are unknown.

———

A loud noise startled the young woman; breaking her daydreams. A young man around her age was fighting against the men in whips that were on guard. His voice was powerful; filled with rage. Miro lowered her head to her knees trying to block out the endless cries. Her young peaceful life has just turned into misery. Whatever was next, sure wasn't anything good, she knew. After a few scuffles with the guards, silence began to overtake the area. The raging young man who she wasn't fond of, turned to everybody yelling "Get up, do something!" The group of Africans were mystified by his courage but didn't move. He was the first to say something on the ship. Everyone was scared, but Miro spoke up.

"Give up, no one is going anywhere." Her blatant response got his attention. The young man glanced at her breathing heavily while she looked up at him. There was an awkward feeling she couldn't explain nor could the young man who stayed silent. He couldn't ignore his heart beating fast. They were in a daze and neither could deny it.

"What do you have to propose?" The young man commented but felt guilty afterward. For the moment, Miro ignored him but after thinking her answer through, she responded,

"There isn't anything to propose. We're at sea with nowhere to go." Miro didn't want to argue. The man didn't appear like one who would take no for an answer either.

"So you're fine with being a captive?" He didn't stop looking at waiting for her. He looked at her intently without blinking. Miro was too tired to keep her eyes open. Her mind traveled back to her father's death which she witnessed. She woke up and said, "Yes, as long as I'm alive." The young man was baffled, not content with her answer. To him, it was strange how she and the others had accepted their fates. When he was ready to respond, three guards entered the cell, two of them grabbing the young man by his arms; keeping him in place while the third took out his whip and struck him on his back with the whip. Miro watched in horror, covering her ears at the young man's cries.

The Tubaabs (White men) laughed "What a bricky man he is." The young man fell on his face and they were kicking him as blood was coming out of his mouth. Then, they exited. Miro had to help him somehow. She crawled over, struggling with the heavy chains on her legs. The young man was on his back not being able to get up,. When he felt her presence, he tried raising.

"Leave me be," he mumbled weakly. She shook her head ripping her cloth apart and wetting it in the bucket nearby. She cleaned his wounds carefully not wanting to cause more pain. It was a painful sight, but she kept on doing it until the blood was almost gone from his back and face. The young man looked up not sure if he could say anything. "What do they call you?" His eyes couldn't move off hers.

"Miro." She answered, smiling weakly. "I go by the name of Osmanu from the Fula tribe." "I'm from the Mandinka." Miro saw Osmanu as a courageous soul and somehow grew a liking towards him.

It was strange how the two bonded, almost as if they were soulmates. Osmanu was impressed by her dark beauty. it was the first time he felt a woman's touch

Thirteen weeks had passed since the Africans embarked on this unknown journey. Many had died from sickness or some from malnourishment. Osmanu and Miro had started having little hopes of surviving the voyage. Osmanu gave up on revolting against the guards on Miro's behalf. He had promised himself whenever they reached land, he'd ask Miro to be his wife.

Miro had become sick and Osmanu promised her a better life when they reach the shore. Little to her knowledge, the ship would reach land that very day. Their hopes sparked once the ship came to a halt.

The survivors were visibly exhausted, worn out, and strongest amongst them stood up to see what was happening. Within seconds, the

Tubaabs (White people) came commanding everyone to get up. Osmanu did, but Miro remained on the ground too weak to stand. One black man saw her and didn't waste time pulling her by the hair to forcefully lift her up. Osmanu couldn't bear the sight, pleading for the man to leave her be. Unfortunately, the man kicked him, causing him to stumble back. That pain didn't stop him from getting up to his feet quickly. The biggest was seeing Miro in agony. The man was about to hit him again when one guard shouted, "We need them, Sane Digby alive!"

———

The Africans had seen the light of the day for the first time in months but they wouldn't enjoy it for long. Osmanu accompanied Miro to the deck of the ship where they looked around wondering what was next.

Never before had they seen tall structures built out of limestone. What was stranger was these people dressed in wigs. The women were walking around wearing long dresses that embraced their bodies perfectly in various styles. Many were walking with their mates who wore long coats to their knees and top hats. It was a different world to the Africans who survived the long journey. On the streets, there were wheeled vehicles drawn by horses.

For a moment, the Africans thought they were free and the Tubaabs would leave them somewhere to live peacefully. Those dreams were pushed aside when they were hurried off the ship.

Miro and remaining survivors were lined up on platforms while others resembling the captors were shouting at them. She wondered why they were still being held in chains.

Her people were taken closer to the crowd; some were being led downward and others forced up to remain. Miro saw everyone take turns in inspecting each one of them. She looked to see if Osmanu was around. He was at the end of the group; being held by a white husky man. They had beaten him again.

It was her turn to step up on the wooden dock. Slowly, she approached the stairs and made her way up; standing on the highest plank. In the crowd, stood white-skinned men with women wearing fancy dresses which was something that amazed her momentarily. The man next to her was purchased first. Miro watched as he was being handed over to a white man in a tall brown hat. This is an auction, she realized.

Her breaths grew as she recognized she was being sold to the Tubaabs. Miro turned around spotting Osmanu and yelled out "Osmanu, help me!" in their native language. He was powerless as Miro was purchased by a young white man with a woman who resembled his spouse.

Osmanu's soul burned as he watched in agony; his love was being taken away and there was nothing he could do about it. "Miro!" he cried as he tried to escape the hold of the guards. She was gone and as much as he wanted, he couldn't see where she was going.

The guard whipped repeatedly, and almost beat him to a pulp. The white man returned minutes later after paying for Miro. He saw Osmanu was still on the block and told the guards he's my nigger as well.

Miro was fatigued as she was brought inside an unfamiliar residence. She was guided by two girls who resembled Senegalese to an old black woman who surprisingly spoke Wolof and explained what their roles were in the house. Miro listened carefully fearing she'd get whipped. The girls were told their duties on the plantation and after they were finished, they'd prepare dinner for their owners, Master William, and his wife.

Miro wondered about Osmanu and worried if he was being tortured again or perhaps dead. Never seeing him again was a strong likelihood. Miro became close with the young man in the weeks leading up to the landing and now he's gone out of her life without a trace.

Dolly, an old black woman mistress, came and gave Miro clothes to change in; one long white dress along with a white kilt and a head wrap. Miro admired the dress as she made her way down to the wooden cabin; a place she would share with the other two Senegalese girls along with Dolly. The cold damp floor collided with her feet once she came inside. There were blankets stacked on the floor and a single board with nails to hang their dresses.

Miro got changed quickly and was ready to go out. Her two roomies came out wearing the same attire. "We haven't properly introduced ourselves," one said. "I'm Keziah." A dark tall girl who looked Senegalese for sure. Her attraction couldn't be denied. Miro kneeled giving her the proper greeting. "I'm Juba." She was shorter and heavier. "We're sisters from Tooba." Miro kneeled again, wishing they hadn't met in such circumstances. "I'm Miro." The girls kneeled and then went to the back of the cabin to gather firewood.

Miro fixed her dress and went outside for the first time, passing the Master's house and seeing his kids playing. It brought back memories of Miro's childhood briefly. She simply ignored them as she kept on walking to the plantation.

Once she arrived, she found she wasn't the only one. There were ten other workers in the yard picking cotton. Miro closed her eyes, internally battling herself whether or not she should accept her fate. For her entire life, she was a fighter.

After several hours of cleaning and picking cotton, Miro was worn out. She felt sick but she knew she had to be patient. She wiped her forehead taking a deep breath while a group of men from a distance caught her attention. Miro was about to resume working when she heard a very familiar voice seeing a blurry figure from afar. She stopped everything. "Osmanu?" She mumbled not quite sure if it was really him. It couldn't be.

Her uncertainty disappeared as the young man approached. Her cotton basket fell to the ground and she ran to him.

Excitement overtook Osmanu as he recognized Miro running towards him. Happiness fulfilled his heart as she jumped in his arms. Their tears fell as they hugged each other tightly, not able to let go. There were no overseers in the area so Osmanu palmed Miro's face admiring her beauty he had missed. Their lips connected incapable to get enough of each other.

"I'm here, and I'm fine my love," said Osmanu. Miro starred but quickly looked around worried if anyone had seen them. There were only Africans around minding their business.

"I thought I'd never see you again." She caressed his face getting lost in his poppy eyes she missed so dearly. Osmanu suddenly turned to look towards the plantation.

"What kind of fate is this?" He was angry. "I could never serve these Tubaab!" His voice grew louder garnering the attention of the others. Miro grabbed his hand lowering her head. "We have no other choice, my love."

"But they have no right to us." Osmanu's face saddened. Miro wanted to say something but was cut off as one worker signaled to them to return to their work before Master came out. Osmanu stepped away from Miro and knew this was how it was going to be. Miro understood and counted it as a blessing that Osmanu was sold to the same master. She didn't care; all she wanted was to be with him.

The day passed quickly as both of them kept

glancing at each other while working. Unable to contain himself, Osmanu kept smiling whenever they made eye contact. Miro, on the other hand, was so timid looking over at him fearing they'd get caught.

The plantation field emptied as the dusk approached and the workers left to do their other duties on the estate. A warm breeze blew across Miro's cheeks and she didn't realize it was Osmanu behind her holding a lily flower. She shook her head beaming and taking it. Miro loved his passionate side but always knew the fighter was in him.

Suddenly, she remembered she had to prepare dinner back at the house. She ran after returning the flower to Osmanu and waved at him when she entered inside.

———

Dolly's look was menacing as Miro entered. Juba and Keziah were cutting up vegetables while the old woman was preparing bread. "Where were you?" Dolly asked, staring down Miro.

"Out in the plantation."

"Go get the table ready." Miro went and gathered dishes from one of the cupboards.

The design on the plates made her pay attention to every color imprinted. Her foot became caught on the high entrance of the door and the dishes fell colliding on the floor. Its pieces were scattered throughout the hallway and Miro stood in shock. Her heart raced as the three women came hooting in horror. Miro knew she had to pick up the pieces quickly. In the process, she'd cut her arm.

"Goodness! My dining set!" Miro closed her eyes shut hearing the Master's wife come into the entrance. She was caught in the act but now there were repercussions.

The woman dragged Miro out, causing her to slip on the dirty ground. Miro's eyes teared knowing what was about to take place.

"Fifteen lashes, you unworthy swine!" screamed Master's wife not wasting any time whipping Miro. The lashes didn't hurt at first. Osmanu looked on in desperation. As Miro weakened, her eyes filled with tears after every hit as she stared at him.

He couldn't do anything but watch. The merciless whips didn't come to an end at fifteen and it felt like an eternity as Miro grasped the dirt trying to overlook the pain. The plantation's workers gathered around to watch, and Osmanu was angered seeing they had the guts to look. It could be anyone instead of Miro, he thought.

Juba, Keziah, and Dolly were speechless as they stood beside the Master's wife. They looked at the ground fearful they would be next.

The last whip hurt causing Miro's back to jolt. Her body finally gave in on her. "Nobody touches her, leave her there to rot!" Master's wife yelled turning around and walking back inside.

The workers went about their business. No one dared to disobey Madamee. Nevertheless, Osmanu was the only one who stood near her. He promised he would not leave her ever. His anger within was so much partly because he had to wait hours till Master fell asleep to carry Miro back to the cabin. He knew he'd be whipped or killed if someone saw him in the woman's quarters.

Dolly, Keziah, and Juba didn't mind as he tucked her in bed. Miro was shivering and Osmanu took several minutes comforting her. Dolly apologized to him for not being able to help. Osmanu asked that they keep secret he'd spend the night. They closed the quarters and turn off the lamps.

Laying next to Osmanu, Miro felt his presence later in the night.

By daybreak, the sun peeked through the old windows. Osmanu had overslept and rushed to put his boots on. Miro noticed they were the only ones there. Osmanu hoped he wasn't late for work. His concern was Miro who was sleeping so peacefully he didn't want to wake her. He rushed out the back door and onto the plantation seeing men on horses circling around the workers. There was one wearing fancy clothes and shiny boots.

"How dare you come this late!" The man struck Osmanu on his back. Osmanu ran faster to do his area. He hadn't seen these men before and guessed Master hired them to keep authority over the workers.

———

Nonstop, Osmanu worked until sunset picking cotton. His mind was only on Miro and hope she had felt better. At the end of the shift, Osmanu along with the other workers left to their cabins while the white men got on their horses. He spotted them circling the women's cabin and worried they would do something bad to them. Osmanu stood beside the window waiting to see what the men were going to do. If they did something to Miro, he'd go out to protect his woman. But there was nothing he could do about it.

While he waited, he overheard the men in the cabin talking. "There are no overseers at dawn. What a perfect time to escape!" The conversation gathered his attention and Osmanu turned around. "Escape?" One nodded. "To the North, Osmanu. We need one more person and you would be welcomed." Osmanu didn't give it his words much importance. It was a promise of death. Escaping was useless as the plantation was enormous and there were overseers everywhere. When Osmanu came back to the window, he saw Miro being taken out of her cabin. He balled his fists, desiring to go out and defend her. "Where are they taking her?" He wondered.

"Master probably called her to his quarters," one man said.

"What for?"

"No one ever goes there," another man said.

———

Two overseers took Miro inside to Master's

main quarters on the second floor. She was fearful to look up, afraid she'd see Master's wife again. She knew she was lucky to be alive. The doors swayed open and a man in his 40s was sitting on the end of his desk whom she assumed was Master. It was the first time she'd seen him since the auction.

His blue eyes examined her body while he smiled. "Miro." He said. She looked up ignoring his eyes. "Yes, Master." She answered with fear dripping inside her tone. She remembered yesterday and the pain was still thumping on her back. She hoped he wouldn't whip her. Master sat in his chair, raising his feet on the desk. "Susan went a little out of her way yesterday. I'm sorry." He pulled out a cigar from the drawer and lit it. He was mesmerized by his slave's beauty.

Miro said nothing but she felt him starring and it was uncomfortable. She didn't know what to do. She heard that no slave has ever visited the second floor of the Master's house. In the short time, she's been there he let her in.

"You are in need of a new dress." He saw the blood staining her dress' back.

"It can easily wash off, sir." As Miro spoke,

Master's wife stormed in. She raised her eyebrows at Miro, still angry about her dishes.

"William, what's this slave's business here?" Master William exhaled fed up by her wife's question. "You can retire now, Miro." Miro turned around and walked out. Master and his wife were arguing as she was led downstairs. She found it quite odd Master treated her so nicely in front of Madamee Susan. However, Miro never wanted to step foot in his office again.

CHAPTER 4

The dishes were Miro's responsibility after dinner. She was left alone in the kitchen without her usual helpers, Keziah and Juba. It has been three months since Miro was brought to the plantation. Her hopes for leaving were fading and she began considering this her home.

Her love for Osmanu was still strong, and their outings were still secret. In the last month or so, a few more slaves were brought in; most rebelled against the masters and it wasn't much use.

Once Miro had finished cleaning the rest of the kitchen, she walked down the path to the cabin. At the same time, the carriage of Sir William and Mistress Susan made its way back to the plantation. They were in the city all day running errands, and Susan looked like she had enjoyed her time away; the carriage was loaded with goods.

Sir William started summoning Miro more often about a month ago. It wasn't to her liking but she had no choice. Whenever Osmanu would ask why Miro was cleaning his office for such long periods, she'd lie to keep the peace. Since Miro had shown good conduct, Master appointed her alone to clean and work his mansion and away from the plantation. Miro wasn't happy as it meant she wouldn't see Osmanu as much.

Often every two days, she had time to be with him. She was smiling when a soft tap on the kitchen's window startled her. It was Osmanu. She opened it and immediately, Osmanu spoke.

"Tonight after the sun sets." She already knew what he meant but was happy that he remembered to remind her. Then, he left waving goodbye.

"Who were you talking to?" Madamee Susan came in the kitchen looking out the window. Miro quickly cleared her throat. "No one, Madamee." Susan looked at her unconvinced. "Retire, your work is done here for today." Miro nodded and left the kitchen.

As she was leaving, she heard the other

girls taking about there were important guests coming to the plantation tomorrow. The girls had been working long hours cleaning the guesthouses for the past week. State officials with their wives were visiting the area mainly in hopes of securing their votes for the town's upcoming elections. There was much talk about the North invading and coming down further but no one knew if it was true.

———

The day passed quickly, and by nightfall, Miro got up after a long rest and got dressed. She wore the new floral dress that Dolly had brought from the city. Miro thought Master might have bought it for her but Dolly quelled that notion. Miro was on her way to an area behind the men's plantation with a small lantern, constantly looking back.

As she neared, she noticed Osmanu in the dark, carrying an even bigger lantern. Both smiled as they shared a deep kiss not letting go of one another.

"I missed you," Osmanu whispered kissing her forehead.

"We almost got caught." Osmanu looked confused and Miro explained.

"Madamee Susan came in right after you left."

Osmanu chuckled. "Allah is always on our side." They proceeded to a tree and sat. Osmanu noticed her new dress. "You look beautiful."

"Dolly brought it from the city." She smiled and Osmanu felt its cloth. He was upset he couldn't get the gifts Miro wanted.

"I miss being a free man. I have lost all of my honor here." She took a hold of his arm, caressing it, wondering what life they'd have if they weren't slaves. Miro imagined her own plantation and children. *What the Tubaabs had done was so inhumane.*

"Let's run away to the North, Miro." He turned toward her getting her attention. Miro shook her head. "You want us to die, Osmanu, we can't." She pulled away slightly.

"We can't live here for the rest of our lives!" "What choice do we have?" Her tone matched his.

"We barely made it here. Our chances of escape with all these Tubaabs watching is almost impossible."

"You said almost. Miro, we must take our chances now. I know somebody who could help us."

They sat silently for a few seconds until Miro spoke. "Promise me you'll remain alive." Her pitch was encouraging, and that was all it took for Osmanu to begin plotting their freedom.

Later in the evening when she returned home, she prayed to Allah both could escape the unbearable place they now call home.

CHAPTER 5

Miro was up before sunrise and knew her chores as they awaited the guests. Master's office was the first place to be cleaned. It was quiet in the house and she assumed all were asleep as she made her way inside. But Master William had awoken early, with one thing on his mind - To make Miro his mistress.

Miro was dusting his desk, wiping away all dirt from the previous day. She hadn't noticed Master come inside; his footsteps were light. Suddenly, he grabbed Miro from behind, lunging her buttocks to his penis area.

Hysteria overtook her when she noticed it was Master. His head was planted in her neck and his grip around got tighter. "Master, no. Please," Miro pleaded. He ignored, as his hands went up her dress creeping towards her vaginal area. Her eyes watered knowing what was about to occur. She was going to lose her virginity. "I've always wanted to do this with a nigger girl like you." His breath was stinking and his hands were now rubbing her breasts invading her solitude. He already touched her most sacred part and stuck his finger inside. Master began stroking her right breast while his other hand was in between her thighs; his rough touch made her wail in pain. "Don't worry, you'll get used to it. Your nigger moans will be heard throughout this house."

"No, please, Master." *The looks she'd get from the others was enough shame. What about Osmanu? How could she even look him in the eyes after this? And what would happen to him if he finds out, would Master take out his anger on him.*

"I can only imagine the look on your boy, Osmanu's face; his precious Miro been deviled by his Master. And he can't do anything about it". Master spoke as if he was reading her mind. "I'll make sure he knows I fucked his woman." Then Master, squeezed her neck, making Miro unable to breathe.

"Please, Master, stop."

"Stop resisting! or would you like Keziah to take your place?". "I own you!"

No! He wouldn't, not Keziah. Miro couldn't allow that; to let this bastard destroy her virginity at the age of twelve even though if it meant taking hers.

This hurt more than the whippings. Master had penetrated her causing bruising. He held her down on the table and Miro's pleas didn't faze him. He kept enjoying himself while Miro tried not to cry.

Minutes later, footsteps could be heard coming down the hall and Master quickly straightened himself. "Don't you say a thing or I'll kill you." Miro, shocked, couldn't utter a syllable. She lowered her dress and left out of the side door of his office before Madamee came.

She was in pain with every step she took to get back to the cabin.

The younger girls were working on the plantation that morning and Miro was relieved no one was inside. She broke down in tears; pulling on her hair, hating herself for letting him do that. Master William took her soul and she wasn't sure if she could keep this secret.

Miro hoped he wouldn't come and see her

like this as it would kill him. As much as she loved Osmanu, she didn't felt she didn't deserve to be his love anymore. Miro spent most of the morning weeping believing she had failed them both.

Four weeks had passed and Miro was holding back behind the farce that had been created. It was tough on her to work at the Master's house, and she tried her best to avoid him. She couldn't bring herself to tell Osmanu, who was still plotting for them to run away to the North. He talked about it endlessly and Miro got tired of hearing it. But after the unwanted encounter with Master, she was undecided about leaving.

Osmanu sensed something was wrong with Miro as the weeks went by. She often made excuses why they couldn't meet and tried avoiding him on the plantation. They didn't gather in their usual spot for a while as Miro claimed she was exhausted from working so much. Osmanu was determined to find out what's bothering her but he knew it wasn't the right time.

One evening, Miro was serving dinner alongside Dolly. She placed the food and utensils on the table for the Masters of the plantation. As usual, she tidied up the kitchen before Master William and Madamee Susan came to sit. Dolly was in the kitchen sweeping the floor and when Miro grabbed a bucket of water, her head twisted in an unusual manner causing her to fall and fainted.

Dolly, Keziah, and Juba came quickly and took her to the cabin. They didn't want Master William or his wife to see Miro ill. They laid her on the floor and were scared as to why that happened. Minutes later, when Miro opened her eyes, they kneeled down, trying to help her. As they came closer, she vomited.

Dolly ordered the girls to clean it up right away pondering what could be the cause. When the girls finished, they rushed back to Sir William's house to attend to their masters.

"Are you late Miro?" Dolly asked calmly. Miro looked up and said, "Yes." The fear from her voice required no other explanation.

"My God!"

For the past week, Miro was feeling sick

almost every day and didn't say a word. She was slow doing her chores but no one noticed.

"You're pregnant." When Dolly said those words, Osmanu had crept inside the cabin hearing the conversation. It was a shock to him. "What did you say?" Miro panicked as Osmanu came to her side looking at Dolly waiting for an explanation.

"That can't be true," Miro uttered, straightening herself.

"The signs are obvious, congratulations."Dolly smiled but there was nothing to smile about.

The baby wasn't Osmanu's and even if it was, he wouldn't be able to father it. Dolly heard what happened that day as she passed by fetching water. She heard Miro moaning lowly in Master's quarters that morning. Sadly, no one could do anything about it.

Dolly told Keziah and Juba when they returned to leave the cabin, giving Osmanu and Miro time.

Osmanu was crushed and began prancing around the room.

"Now, we have a reason to leave." Miro couldn't look at him. She remained on the ground, thinking about the baby and how it was a curse. "We can still be a family, my love,."

"I'm pregnant, Osmanu." As much as it pained, it wasn't a secret anymore. Osmanu pulled his hand from hers. He thought he heard wrong but Miro had repeated, "It's the Master's." She looked at him, so sorry for what had happened.

"You're lying." Osmanu's eyes were watery. He couldn't believe it. "How are you pregnant?"

Miro explained what happened at Master's office and she pleaded for him to stop but he wouldn't. She also wanted Osmanu to live a happy life without her, and completely forget about her. They wouldn't be happy even if she could run away with him. The baby would be a permanent reminder of the Master, which took away Osmanu's most beloved.

Moments later after continually prancing the room, Osmanu became distant. His heart was shattered by the woman he loved so dearly.

He took one last look, without saying a thing and left from the cabin. His journey to the North away from this horrid place would began immediately. Miro knew he would leave that night, and it would be the last time she'd ever see him. She accepted the fate of spending the rest of her life on Sir William's plantation without ever being free.

———

As her stomach grew and others noticed, Miro earned the title as the Mistress of the Master. The gossip spread quickly around the estate about Miro. Madamee's anger was so much that she tried to killing her but stopped short of it when Master confessed his infidelity. He told Susan he was sorry and the devil made him do it that morning.

It was rumored that Osmanu was alive and almost to the North with two others who ran away from the plantation.

Two years later, Miro heard Osmanu became a doctor, got married and had two children already. More slaves were brought to Sir William's plantation. The void in Miro's heart couldn't be filled with Osmanu gone. It would stay there forever, as a sign of what she had left of good.

———

The household of the Addington family, now

had a boy, Robin Addington, the son of William and Miro. This caused Madamee to ultimately leave her husband after she could fathom seeing little Robin day after day. Madamee Susan never had children with William Addington and she remarried years later. In the meantime, Miro forced herself to love this innocent creature since it was hers.

Dolly, Keziah, and Juba being the faithful workers they always had been, stood by Miro's side through the hell of being with Master. When Master wanted sex, he'd give little Robin to Dolly and the girls to take care of. Miro would remember Osmanu as her only love as Master made love to her. She'd just lay there, reminiscing about the man who fought on the slaveship.

As much as Osmanu had hated Miro deep inside, he never forgot about her even though he was happily married in the North. He hoped that once the War was over, he'd be the person who'd rescue Miro from the tyranny. One thing they forever knew, their futures would be a lot better in the end.